Richard Homer Garnett

**Iphigenia in Delphi. A dramatic Poem.**

Richard Homer Garnett

**Iphigenia in Delphi. A dramatic Poem.**

ISBN/EAN: 9783743358775

Manufactured in Europe, USA, Canada, Australia, Japa

Cover: Foto ©Andreas Hilbeck / pixelio.de

Manufactured and distributed by brebook publishing software
(www.brebook.com)

Richard Homer Garnett

**Iphigenia in Delphi. A dramatic Poem.**

Iphigenia in Delphi

# IN SAME SERIES.

*Orestes at the Altar of Delphi.*

# Iphigenia in Delphi

*A DRAMATIC POEM*

With Homer's "Shield of Achilles,"
and other Translations
from the Greek

by
RICHARD GARNETT

CAMEO SERIES

T. FISHER UNWIN     PATERNOSTER SQ.
LONDON E.C.   MDCCCXC.

# Dramatic.

# Iphigenia in Delphi.

## DRAMATIS PERSONÆ.

Hermes.

Iphigenia.

Electra.

Orestes.

Eurycles.

An Attendant *on Iphigenia.*

Apollo.

The Shade of Achilles
  (*a mute personage*).

# The Argument.

AN oracle declared that Iphigenia, daughter
of Agamemnon, King of Mycenæ, must
be sacrificed to Artemis, to procure a passage
to Troy for the Grecian fleet lying becalmed
at Aulis. Iphigenia was brought to Aulis
under pretence of a marriage with Achilles,
and was about to be put to death when
Artemis substituted a hind in her place, and
conveyed her to Tauris in Scythia, where she
became priestess. The Greeks believed that she
had been actually sacrificed, and it was partly in
revenge for this deed that Agamemnon was
murdered on his return from Troy by his wife
Clytemnestra. When Agamemnon's son
Orestes had grown up, he took vengeance on
Clytemnestra and her paramour Ægisthus by
the help of his sister Electra; and then,
being persecuted by the Furies on account of
the death of his mother, repaired to Delphi to

ask counsel of Apollo. He was directed to go
to Tauris and carry off the statue of Artemis.
In this he succeeded by the aid of Iphigenia,
and returned in her company to Delphi, to be
purified from the murder of Clytemnestra.
Meanwhile Electra, who was ignorant of the
existence of Iphigenia, had also repaired to
Delphi to inquire respecting the fate of her
long absent brother, and to consecrate the axe
with which Clytemnestra had slain Agamemnon, and with which she had in turn been
destroyed by Orestes.

SCENE.—*The Temple of Apollo at Delphi. A fire is burning on the centre of the altar.*

HERMES (*conducting the Shade of Achilles*).

How should the world's great edifice subsist,
But by appointed ministries of Gods,
Power multiplied, one Form of many names,
In heaven and hell and earth-embracing sea?
Therefore I, Hermes, have my rightful place,
And sway usurped not by another God,
But to myself peculiar, so that thou,
My glorious brother, Lord of light and song,
Phœbus, wert fain to invoke my ministry,
Saying, "O fleetest, from whose hands I erst
Received the lyre whose melody doth make
More godlike the festivity of Gods,
And whom for recompense I did equip
With the caduceus, by whose might thou art prince
    prince
And marshaller of all the airy shades,

I pray thee, use it for my service now.
Go, seek the realms by no celestial God
Traversed save thee, arising from the obscure
Of Stygian gulfs profoundest on the plain
Elysian, where the great Achilles pines.
Aye, pines, for well thou knowest that not
　　amid
The sweetness of undying asphodel
Can rest the spirit of its right divine
Frustrate on earth and in Elysium.
And therefore hath he ever sat apart,
Moody and undelighted to converse
With them who won the Fleece, or whom the
　　plain
Of Thebes entombed, or himself with strenuous
　　arm
Slew or avenged around the ramparts vast
Immortals laboured for Laomedon.
Nay, but he shuns Patroclus! Even for this,
That she, at whose behest the night is clear
Or dim with her pure emblem's wax or wane,
Artemis, my chaste sister, bore away
Iphigenia, daughter of the King
Of Argolis, from all the flowery troops
Of Grecian maids elected for his bride.
But I, remembering how Achilles forced

The violent Agamemnon to restore
Chryseis to her sire, priest of my shrine
Sminthian, thus to stay the ravage of shafts
Dreadfully speeding from my silver bow ;
Have pity on him, decreeing that this day,
Here in this Delphian sanctuary, where most
Divine is breathed my oracular might, before
The starry sequence of nocturnal hours,
Iphigenia shall be his again.
But go, the rest shall be a care to me."
Therefore I went, and with the heroic birth
Of Thetis silver-footed have returned ;
Giving him once again to see the sun ;
And Æther, milk of life to mortal men
To quaff well-pleased ; in these omniscient halls
Hovering a shade all-seeing and unseen ;
And, witting of the issue, not the way,
To wait on destiny's accomplishment,
Expectant, yet, as suits the scholar of Death,
Serene in observation unperturbed,
Knowing that nought is done without the Gods,
And knowing that the Gods do all things well.

    [*They disappear.* Iphigenia *and the* Atten-
        dant *come forward.*

        Attendant.

Bethink thee, princess, of the Aulian fane,

And altar where thou, victim-filleted,
Didst sob a helpless girl, whose limbs relaxed
Rough hands sustained ; and with thy hair
    drawn back
Another's hand entwined, exposing all
The agonising neck to the bare knife,—
When lo ! a Voice, and in thy place a hind !
Shall not the Gods who guarded then guard
    now ?

IPHIGENIA.

They saved me haply for Orestes' sake.
Who seeks the fallen blossom when the fruit
It heralded hangs ripe in rounded gold ?

ATTENDANT.

Seest thou, then, peril, or the sign of it ?

IPHIGENIA.

No more than when I went to wed Pelides,
Or wove the fillet for Orestes' head !
The Immortals need not, when they launch
    their shafts,
The ambush of a cloud.

ATTENDANT.

                A pair divine,
Apollo, I have heard, and Artemis,
Erst with avenging arrows smote and slew
Her progeny, who with irreverent speech

Outraged Latona, and now stands, a stone,
On Sipylos, distilling clammy tears ;
But neither priestess unto Artemis
Was Niobe, nor have I ever heard
Iphigenia wrong with lip unschooled
The Gods, unless in deeming them to make
No difference 'twixt the sinner and the just.

IPHIGENIA.

Am I not then a sinner, who have fled
Artemis' altars, I her minister ?
And robbed her of her sacrifice, and snatched
Her image away, and made her fane a void ?

ATTENDANT.

Nay, verily, for thou hast given her Greece !
Free offerings for servile, lyres for drums,
And cheerful rites for savage butcheries.

IPHIGENIA.

It may be so, and yet will I beseech
Apollo, lest an evil come of it.
O Phœbus, is it not an augury
Of good, that Fate hath led me to thy shrine
Whom most of all the Gods I should implore ?
For, when division anciently was made
Above, and each Immortal took his own,
'Twas given to thee to be our human kind's
Enlightener and healing comforter.

Thou showest thyself, and the benighted earth
Is splendid, and the drowsy hand resumes
The necessary task ; thou signallest,
And incense straight goes up to all the Gods.
Thou measurest the year, the earth is drest
By thee in all her seasonable garbs ;
Yea, even thy departing beam inflames
Innumerable lights, the moon walks forth
Clad in the pure redundance of thy ray.
By thee the herbage prospers, and the trees,
And herds, and flocks thyself hast shepherded,
Serving the throne Thessalian.    In thy name
Men rear the citied homes of wealth and law,
And walls rise high with battlements and
     towers.
Moreover thou by wisest oracles
Dost make the future present, and hast found
Medicine, leniment of corporal pangs,
And Music, the assuager of the soul.
And, taught of thee, the sacred minstrels sing
Civility, and pious rites, and love,
And all that makes man loveable to man.
Needs must thou then hate all barbarity,
All jealousy and jarring dissonance,
All blood and vengeance, all the cloud of grief
That folds a kinsman for a kinsman slain.

And righteously then thou didst avert
Thy face erewhile in Argolis, and make
Thy radiant car invisible, and all
The earth a darkness, when my grandsire—O
The horror, and the fortune of our house !
O be it spent ! and may a younger race
Entreat thee for an unwithholden boon !
I plead not my own woes.   I do not urge
The Aulian altar or the Scythian years,
Or even remind thee how thou promised'st
Orestes lustral purity, and peace
From madness, and proclaim that it befits
The God to keep the promise of the God.
But rather would I say, with simple speech,
I have a brother, thou a sister, God !
Artemis, huntress virginal, whose car
Is glory of lone night, as thine of day.
If thou lov'st her as I Orestes (else
Thou God wert less than man, since well 'tis
     sung,
Divine and human needs must love alike,
The human being divine oppressed with bonds,
Divine the human in glad liberty),
Then, I adjure thee, aid him ! set him free
From spasm and panic, lead him to his throne
Ancestral, granting me to sit with him

Far through the lengthening years in quiet
    seats ;
And with us she who saved him, greatly took
The stain of half his fault, my sister dear
Electra, whom not having seen I love.

ATTENDANT.

O princess, be it to thy brother and thee
Even as thou desirest from the God !

    [ELECTRA, *carrying an axe, appears at the*
        *entrance to the temple.* IPHIGENIA *and*
        *the* ATTENDANT *withdraw towards the*
        *back of the scenes.*]

ELECTRA.

O thou earth-centre where in olden time
Met the strong eagle-twain dismissed by Zeus,
This from the east, that from the western
    verge :
Altar, what suppliant hails thee with a heart
Grateful as mine ?  For as one grasps a plank,
Sole stable thing in the dissolving sea,
Clasped thee Orestes ; at thy precinct fell
His frenzy from his soul, before thee paused
With grinded teeth the baffled dogs of hell.
And now would I make question——

    [IPHIGENIA *comes forward.*]
                 But methinks

Another—Artemis ! were thine this fane,
Or bore this form of aspect blanched and
    mild
Quiver or crescent, she were deemed of me
Thy statue, animate, unpedestalled.

           IPHIGENIA.

Surely she is the daughter of a king !

           ELECTRA.

What if she be the fateful Pythia's self ?

           IPHIGENIA.

My heart to hers cries inarticulately.

           ELECTRA.

The tongue my love would loose, my awe
    restrains.

           IPHIGENIA.

Yet why do I delay to question her ?—
Thou stately one, art thou, then, sprung from
    Troy ?

           ELECTRA.

Ill greet'st thou me with an abhorrèd word.

           IPHIGENIA.

Thou look'st so noble and so sorrowful.

           ELECTRA.

What, then ? Delay not to unfold thy thought.

           IPHIGENIA.

I deemed that haply in captivity——

ELECTRA.

O enviable to mine the captive's lot!

IPHIGENIA.

Hath Ilion wrought thee, then, such wretched
doom?

ELECTRA.

Sire, sister, mother, brother, all she took.

IPHIGENIA.

Thou speak'st an unintelligible word.

ELECTRA.

Wherefore? How is my speech incredible?

IPHIGENIA.

Fathers may fall, fighting in Ares' fields—

ELECTRA.

Mine sought the Styx by a more dismal
road.

IPHIGENIA.

But sisters, mothers, how shall these be
slain?

ELECTRA.

Forbear, thrust not thy fingers in my wounds.

IPHIGENIA.

Forgive me; I have known wounds' anguish,
too.

ELECTRA.

Unfortunate, what, then, hath been thy
pang?

IPHIGENIA.

The captive's doom thou deemest enviable.

ELECTRA.

O were it mine, were but my brother safe!

IPHIGENIA.

Thou hast a brother, then.　What fate is his?

ELECTRA.

'Twere best he weltered on the uneasy main.

IPHIGENIA.

O miserable, if this indeed the best!

ELECTRA.

Else much I fear his limbs, repast of kites——

IPHIGENIA.

Lie unentombed on some barbaric strand?

ELECTRA.

Where never shall a sister bury them.

IPHIGENIA.

I pray the Gods to send ye happier doom.

ELECTRA.

Why weepest thou?　Thou hast a brother,
　then?

IPHIGENIA.

Whose presence every instant I await.

ELECTRA.

O happy thou!　What need of further bliss!
But I have come to entreat the God for mine.

#### IPHIGENIA.

Then will I leave thee, deeming not the God
Demands a listener at his conference ;
And only say, may he be favourable !

[IPHIGENIA *retires;* ELECTRA *lays the axe
on the altar.*

Detested instrument of infamy !
Well pleased, I lay thee now where ne'er
   shall man
Uplift thee for our misery again.
Another word was mine, O axe, what time
I gave thee to Orestes' hand, and said,
" Seest thou this rust ?  It is thy father's blood,
Till thou efface it with another stain."
And now it is my mother's ; and whose next ?
Knowest thou, Latona-born, prophetic God ?
Ah me ! how I mistrust thy oracle,
Which said to Agamemnon's son, " Go forth,
And, where the inhospitable billow beats
Sullen on Tauris, and a bloody steam
Wavers around the effigy severe
Of Artemis, my sister, do thou seize
That image, hither bear it, and have rest."
Gladly he heard, and his sea-cleaving bark
Equipped with mast, and sail, and oar, and
   bench

Where many a comrade sat ; and in his face
Glowed ardour like a racer's when he sees
Near and more near the distinguishable goal.
And I beside the billow stood, and waved
My veil, while mist, born spray-like from the
     bright
Wild fluctuation of my smiles and tears,
Concealed the diminution of his sails.
But, Phœbus, morn by morn thou issuest forth,
A splendour pacing in four-steeded car,
With light displaying nothing that I love,
And warmth that cannot dry a tear of mine.
And eve by eve thou duly dost commit
Thy chariot to thy Hour, whose silvery star
Smiles on thy forfeit pledge—and thou a God !
Yet, haply, thou wert true to happier men ;
But our sad house, the refuge of all crime,
Where son with mother wars, with husband
     wife,
Brother with brother ; wherefore should the
     Gods
Deal with us as we deal not with ourselves?
Ah me !
          Orestes, is my anguish all my own ?
If, as I trust, thy effort hath prevailed
To win the statue, and thou bear'st it home

In strong sea-furrowing galley, dost thou muse,
"How shall one subtly, with ambiguous
    speech,
Prepare Electra, lest she die of joy?"
Or if, alas! alas! thou hast stood forlorn
For slaughter in that fane, was then thy
    thought,
" Alas, for my Electra when she hears!"?
Indeed I know not, but too well I know
Sooner a girl shall slay a weaponed man
Than man love woman with a woman's love.

EURYCLES (*entering the temple*).

Daughter of Agamemnon, turn and hear
A heavy word from a reluctant tongue.

ELECTRA.

Who art thou, man? whence sent? what
    thing to tell?

EURYCLES.

One of Orestes' comrades, bound with him
To Scythia—bound without him back to
    Greece.

ELECTRA.

Without! without! thou darest not to call
    Orestes dead!

EURYCLES.

I have not seen him die.

### ELECTRA.

Then animate?   Thou darest to be mute!

### EURYCLES.

O princess, listen only to my tale,
And I will tell thee truly all I know.

### ELECTRA.

Speak quickly, while I yet have life to hear.

### EURYCLES.

Long did the north wind baffle, but at length
We gained the coast of massacre, and found
A cave low-arched, wave-whispering at its
      mouth,
But vaulted loftily within, and dry.
Therein we entered, and with food and drink
Refreshed ourselves ; and then Orestes spake,
" Rest here, my friends, while Pylades with me
Goes forth to explore this region what it is,
And how the Goddess' image may be won."
And so they parted, venturous ; but the hours
Wore on ; nor came there any sign from
      them.
Then took we counsel, and cast forth a lot
For perquisition, and it fell on me.
Then went I forth, and found an open space
Before a moated city, and in it
Pylades and thy brother standing bound ;

Their armour rent from them, their dress
    defiled
With blood and dust, and from the brow of
    each
Oozed the thick sullen droppings, and I
    judged
Our friends the booty of a multitude,
Beset by rustics armed with clubs and stones,
And turned me round to fly, but as I turned
Came forth a wondrous woman tall and fair,
Grecian in aspect, in a Grecian garb
Draping her stateliness symmetrical.
And truly I had deemed her Artemis ;
But that, the while she approached and shore
    a lock
From either captive, thundering pealed acclaim
Exultant from the barbarous multitude,
"The priestess, who shall give the men to
    death ! "
I turned and fled, and flying saw her still.
And hastening to our ambush I called forth
My comrades to the rescue, but alas !
One said, How shall we brave a host in arms ?
And one, The slaughter is performed ere this.
And one, The Pythian but fulfils his pledge,
What peace is peaceful as the peace of death ?

And so we sailed.   Alas! regard me not
So rigidly with thy dismaying eyes!
For verily, had I prevailed, thou hadst heard
Thy brother's fortunes from thy brother's lips,
Or never from the lips of any man.

### ELECTRA.

I hate thee not, but get thee from my sight.

### EURYCLES.

I go as thou commandest, yet not far ;
Full surely thou wilt soon have need of me.

[*Goes out.*

### ELECTRA.

Now see I all the blindness of our race,
Now see I all the malice of the Gods.
O my Orestes ! O my brother ! now
A mangled victim ! who could e'er conceive
The time to have been  when thou didst come
        a swift
Avenger, terrible and beautiful,
Yet cloaked with craft, unrecognisable,
Bearing the urn  thou feignd'st to contain thy
        dust ?
And I believed, and took it to my arms,
And wept such tears as I am shedding now,
But then did never deem  to shed again ;
Till thy dear heart was melted, and thy arms

Met sudden round my neck, and thou didst
   cry,
"Believe it not, Electra, but believe
Thou clasp'st the living brother, not the
   dead,"
Who had not deemed me mad had I rejoined,
"I would, Orestes, that the tale were true...
Yet, had it been true, then hadst thou
   obtained
Decorous rites of sepulture most meet,
Paid by a kindred hand, thy sister had
   warmed
Thy chill ash for a little with her breast,
And then avenged it. Yea, this hand had
   reeked
And dripped with the adulterous blood, thou
   pure,
And I sole quarry of the hounds of hell."
Ah me! the gladness I was glad to lose!
What sudden thought grasps and enkindles
   me?
The wheel of circumstance brings all things
   back.
Again thou diest, my brother, and again
My vengeance lives. Alas! I cannot go,
And with this hatchet cleave thy hateful head,

And spill thy abominable blood, accursed
Vassal of Artemis.   But thou, false God,
Smooth murderer with ambiguous oracles,
Thou art not safe as thou esteem'st thyself.
Look  down,  and  thou  shalt  see  to  what  a
    deed
A desperate heart can prompt a daring hand.
Forsake thy nectared and ambrosial feast,
And save thy shrine, if thou art indeed a God !
          [*Snatches a brand from the altar.*

IPHIGENIA (*entering*).
Ha, wretched, what art doing with that brand ?

ELECTRA.
I fire the fane of a deceitful God.

IPHIGENIA.
Nay, truly, if this hand can hinder thee.

ELECTRA.
Thou would'st then rather I should burn thy
    eyes !

IPHIGENIA.
Apollo will protect his combatant.

ELECTRA.
Ah me ! the brand is caught out from my
    grasp.

IPHIGENIA.
Thou seest, the weak are strong by piety.

C

### Electra.

O miserable slave of the Unjust !
May these requite thee, abject, with the doom
Bestowed by them upon the brave and free !
Thou hast a brother ?—may'st thou see him die !
A sister ?—may'st thou slay her with thy
    hand !

### Iphigenia.

Curse, frantic, with a curse I do not heed ;
For surely thou art crazed with wretchedness.

### Electra.

O maiden, as a mother who has lost
Daughter or son, clasps the insensible urn,
And fondles it, and feigns it is her child—
So thee, though thou art colder than an urn,
Yet will I feign another, and will make
Thee umpire of my quarrel with the Gods.
I had, alas ! alas ! a brother ; his name
Thou knowest not, nor shalt.  Suffice, he
    turned
Hither, inquiring of his death or life.
Now, had the God said "death," who would
    have blamed ?
But it was little for my brother to die,
Unless the Gods could have their sport with
    him,

So he was told, "Find such and such, and
    rest."
He went to find it, and he found the grave.
Now, if I stood and railed, the God would
    say,
" What rest so deep as the grave's quietude ? "
O base, contemptible, and lying God !
I see thou chokest with thy zeal to earn
The wages of thy supple abjectness.
Come, plead thy masters' cause, and be repaid
With some reward unenviable by me.

IPHIGENIA.

Alas ! for all thy solemn hierarchy,
Olympus, and the Order that controls
The world, had Love dominion for an hour !
But this was craft and wisdom of the Gods,
That, knowing Love by nature masterful,
Inconstant, wilful, proud, tyrannical,
They compassed him with all fragility,
Set him at subtlest variance with himself,
Stronger than Change or Death, than Time
    that leaves
The storied bronze with unengraven front,
Yet weak as weakness' self ; nor weak alone,
But without weakness inconceivable.
Say now we grant it were impossible

Thy brother should perish, had I found thee
    here
Asking the God for him with thy wild voice?
Thou buyest not Love save with the anxious
    heart,
That quakes at what *may* happen—often *must;*
Else were thy love as empty as thy fear.

#### ELECTRA.

Methinks I hear the main's inhabitant
Marvelling why the foolish seaman drowns.
Thy brother is alive, and mine is dead.

#### IPHIGENIA.

'Tis for that thing I pity thee, and now
Would offer thee a sister in his room.

#### ELECTRA.

Thee for a sister, heartless! Say as soon
Artemis' image, or her cruel self;
Or even her satellite, the murderess.

#### IPHIGENIA.

Alas! thou knowest not what thou dost reject.
But why curse Artemis? 'tis her I serve.

#### ELECTRA.

Thou servest Artemis! Had I but known!
Off! off! detested!

#### IPHIGENIA.

Whence this frantic rage?

ELECTRA.

Off! ere I smite thee! Thou my sister, thou!

IPHIGENIA.

Again I warn thee that thou dost reject,

Thou knowest not what. A sister's were a
breast

Whereon to weep, venting in rainy tears

The fury thou amassest now in clouds,

And hurlest at the Gods in thunderbolts.

ELECTRA.

Hear then, I had a sister, and have not.

IPHIGENIA.

Wretched, by what calamity deprived?

ELECTRA.

A Mighty One (inquire not for her name)

Looked upon her, and thought—How beautiful!

Simple, and sweet, and innocent, and blithe

With buoyant life, yet must the virgin die,

For I have some strange pleasure in her
death;

Wherefore she took the maid, and slaughtered
her.

IPHIGENIA.

Thou talkest idly, grief hath turned thy
brain.

Ah, me ! thy eyes blaze, and a fire of light
Is poured upon thee all from head to foot.

ELECTRA.

Sister, ere me a victim of the Unjust,
Leave ghostly Acheron, if thou canst, awhile,
And see how thy beloved avenges thee !
(*Snatches a brand from the altar.*)

IPHIGENIA.

Madwoman cease ! ah, me ! help ! rescue !
help !

EURYCLES (*running in*).

What means this clamour and commotion ?
(*perceiving* IPHIGENIA).
Gods !

ELECTRA.

Thou palsiest me with look unspeakable.

EURYCLES.

Behold thy brother's murderess !

IPHIGENIA.

I ? I ?

EURYCLES.

The Scythian woman, vowed to Artemis !

ELECTRA.

Kind Gods, I do not curse ye any more.
(*Snatches the axe from the altar, and strikes*
IPHIGENIA.)

Die, hatefullest !          [IPHIGENIA *falls.*

                    O, drunkenness of joy !

Aye, moan.   Thy moans are music to mine
     ears.

              ORESTES (*entering*).

Eyes ? what do ye behold ?

                    ELECTRA.

Orestes !

                    EURYCLES.

Prince !

                    ELECTRA.

O day of happiness !   O crown of life !

Orestes ! clasp—

                    ORESTES.

Off ! off ! abominable !

O temple, fall upon us ! bury us !

Electra ! wretch detestable !

              IPHIGENIA.

              Electra !

Hasten and kiss me ere it be too late.

(*Dies.*   ORESTES *throws himself upon the body.*)

                    EURYCLES.

The Gods be thanked, there yet is time to fly.

                         [*Escapes.*

              ELECTRA.

Orestes, to this sudden shock of joy

My whole frame thrills responsive, my full
    heart's
Glad clamour in my bosom silences
All dissonancy, and I do not ask
How here? how sped? how saved? how taken
    for lost?
Or why thou spurnest my embrace, the while
Thou kneelest to caress a murderer.

      ORESTES (*not regarding* ELECTRA).

O speak, look, make some sign, or only
    breathe!

          ELECTRA.

How, when thou deign'st no look or word
    to me?

          ORESTES.

Thou slayest me, counterfeiting to be slain.

          ELECTRA.

Met ever brother with a greeting like this—

          ORESTES.

Woe! woe! it is most certain she is dead.

                   [*Rising.*

Peace, execrable, red with sister's blood!

          ELECTRA.

Orestes, thou art mad or mockest me.
What ravest thou of sisters and their blood?
Look upon me, thou hast no sister else.

### Orestes.

Too true the word thou spakest then, ac-
   cursed !
Yet rather say I have no sister at all,
For never will I hail thee sister more.

### Electra.

Alas ! alas ! the Fury grasps thee again !
Too long have I perceived thou knowest me
   not.
O hide thee in my bosom, ere she gaze
Thy heart cold with her·petrifying eyes !

### Orestes.

I see indeed a Fury, seeing thee.

### Electra (*to* Iphigenia).

Abominable ! more hateful than I deemed.
Who thought thee but his murderer, for then
Most surely I had kissed him by the Styx.
But thou hast stolen his love away from me,
And how to win it back I do not know.

### Orestes.

Thou sayest well : not the abyss of Acheron
Could part us with a chasm like thy crime.

### Electra.

Why ravest thou, and idly talk'st of crime ?
I have slain who would have slain thee, have
   I not ?

ORESTES.

No, thou hast murdered my deliverer.

ELECTRA.

What ? not the ministrant of Artemis ?

ORESTES.

Yea ; and thy sister, for thy better knowledge.

ELECTRA.

O foolish !   Deem'st thou her Chrysothemis ?

ORESTES.

Chrysothemis sleeps sound in Argive earth.

ELECTRA.

And all men know Iphigenia slain
At Aulis, by the vengeful Artemis.

ORESTES.

Thou art near the mark ; yet call the place
Delphi, not Aulis, and the murderer of blood
Electra, and no longer Artemis.
For Artemis was merciful, and caught
The victim away in darkness, and the Greeks
Slaughtered a hind, esteeming it the maid.
But she was rapt to Tauris, there became
The priestess of the sanctuary, gave
Me life and sweet return, for herself took death,
For thee, most miserable, fratricide.

ELECTRA.

Apollo, how thou art avenged of me !

## ORESTES.

Woe worth the Gods' inimitable craft
To frame delight from peril and distress,
And utter anguish from felicity !
O sister, o'er whose gashed and prostrate
    corpse
The red blood rushes, smoking like a steed,
How were we happy in the days of toil !
When, spent and dizzy with the uncontrolled
Climbing and lapsing of the clashing brine,
We hailed the expected joy more confidently
Than birds the sure appearing of the morn.
"Orestes," thou wouldst say, ("for I have lost
The memory of the land I left so young),
Come, tell me of our Argos, how it is.
O foolish me, forgetting thou wert torn
Away in younger years than mine, yet thou
Hast seen whom chiefly I desire—Electra !
Describe her; is she liker thee or me ?
O kindest Gods, what greeting will be ours !
How will she marvel whom Orestes brings !
With what inquiry will she scan my face !
With what amazement listen to my tale !
With what enchantment leap into my arms !"
O, fondly has thy sister welcomed thee !
Alas ! I know not whom to pity most,

Thee, murdered, or thee, murderer, or myself,
Robbed of two sisters by one evil blow.

ELECTRA.

Thou sayest well, Orestes.  I am dead ;
Touch not this hand again, press not this lip,
Give me no tears, this corpse demands them
 all.
Speak not one word of pity or of love,
And never call me sister any more.
Only be patient with some sad last words
Before I go away and slay myself.
Think not Iphigenia yearned alone
To greet me.  Often in the dismal nights,
When thou wert far in exile, and our roof
Rang with adulterous revel, and I lay
Hearkening on my lone couch, burning with
 hate
And shame for her who knew no shame, a
 dream
Has stolen upon me, and my sister appeared
Departing for the Aulian armament,
Bashful and joyous, bending to appease
My childish grief : " Farewell till thou dost
 go,
The bride of the most valiant of the Greeks."
And, wakening, I have passionately sobbed,

And smitten upon my couch as though it
were
A sepulchre I summoned to restore
Iphigenia only for an hour.
And I have had my hour, and in my hour
Reviled, outraged, and lastly murdered her
Whom most I loved of mortals after thee.
Orestes, now I go, but hear and mark
My last sad words, as though a spirit spake,
Crave nought intemperately from Gods more
kind
Withholding, haply, than conferring boons.

ORESTES.

Thou didst not crave Iphigenia alone?

ELECTRA.

There was for whom I longed with such
excess——

ORESTES.

That? Haste to tell me, though indeed I
know.

ELECTRA.

The tears I shed for her seemed even relief.

ORESTES.

Thou meanest thy brother surely, or whom
else?

ELECTRA.

To whom else should a wretched sister look?

ORESTES.

O faithful heart, enfolded in these arms—

ELECTRA.

Off! wouldst thou be polluted with this blood ?

ORESTES.

What is pollution like ingratitude ?

ELECTRA.

So guilty, known to all Gods and men !

ORESTES.

So long with thee, and have not kissed thee
    yet !

ELECTRA.

Thou claspest, soothest me, the murderess,
    thou !

ORESTES.

To whom else should a wretched sister look ?

ELECTRA.

Thou dost forget, methinks, whose blood
    this is.

ORESTES.

And thou, whose thou hast kissed from off
    these hands.

ELECTRA.

No murderer thou, but executioner.

ORESTES.

And thou, thou thoughtest to avenge my
    death.

ELECTRA.

Thou wilt be purified, but what of me?

ORESTES.

Thou shalt be purified, or I will not.
But yield thee to my will, resist no more ;
For neither will I suffer thee to die,
Nor quit thee while thou breathest on the
    earth.

[*The temple is illuminated by the sudden
    appearance of* APOLLO. *In the background*
    HERMES *is seen departing with the shades of*
    ACHILLES *and* IPHIGENIA.]

APOLLO.

Orestes, while the man of noble heart
Yet strives with circumstance, the Gods look
    on,
Willing the glory to be all his own ;
But then descend, and take him by the hand
When at the last he shines a conqueror.
So now that thou hast wholly put away
All hatred and revenge and evil thought,
And art most wholly Love's, hear the reward
Of deeds divinely done from lips divine.
And, first, no Fury at thee shall hurl again
Her torch, or lash thee with a snaky lock,
Whom now the purifying vase awaits,

And quiet by my oracles foretold.
And also for Electra there is peace,
Who, deeming to slay an enemy with an axe,
Did set a bride's wreath on a sister's brow.
O ignorance of blind mortality!
For know, it hath been all-constraining Love's
Ancient and solemn counsel, that the bride
Reft from Achilles erst, he should regain,
And rule with her the sacred island-realm
Invisible, inviolate, the home
Of innocent sprites and hero-shades august,
Screened in the secrecy of western seas.
Yet by thy hand must first the hallowed dues
Of sepulture be rendered.   These performed,
My sister's fane at Brauron seek, therein
Instal the Taurian effigy, not now
With carnage placable, but some young maid,
With one warm drop drawn from her throb-
     bing neck,
Shall stain it, nor shall Artemis crave more.
There, too, shalt thou be purged of blood,
     nor less
Electra.   Thence to Argolis return,
And prosperously reign, a kingly life
Proved and accepted ; by stern fate, swift
     change,

Trials and toils and venturous tragic deeds,
Splendid and dark, tempered and sealed for
  sway.

### ORESTES.

O Phœbus, with a glad and grateful mind
Will I accomplish all thou bid'st me do.
A little while, dear shade, and we will come,
And fondly with befitting obsequies
Dismiss thee to the regions of the blest.
Electra, hear'st thou?
Come, grasp my hand; erect thee from the
  earth.

### ELECTRA.

Leave thou me here to grovel where I lie,
And reign in Argolis, forgetting me.

### ORESTES.

I see thou art my Furies' friend, not mine,
Who dost debar me from the lustral fount,
Which never will I seek but by thy side.

### ELECTRA.

O sister, sister, how forsake thy corpse?

### ORESTES.

O sister, sister, how repel my hand?

### ELECTRA.

Thou forcest me, Orestes, I obey;
But know, more easily in Argolis

Did I constrain thee, frantic, to thy couch
Phantasmal, with my kisses making blind
Thy eyes against the serpents, from thy lips
Wiping the foam——

### Orestes.

As I the blood from thee.
Griev'st thou that I repay thee at the last ?
Come, my Electra, we will weep no more ;
Knowing that nought is done without the
    Gods,
And knowing that the Gods do all things well.

# Epic.

# The Shield of Achilles.

THE various shield first framed he, massive,
　　vast.
A gleaming rim around he deftly cast
Of triple plates ; a silver brace, to wield
The orb, contrived ; then fivefold wrought the
　　shield.
Next with embossed device the work o'erlaid,
And Earth, Sea, Sky, with subtle skill por-
　　trayed :
The unwearied Sun, the Moon's perfected light,
All constellations radiant in the height
Of Heaven ; the Pleiads and the Hyad train :
Orion's strength ; the Pole-encircling Wain,
Orion's watcher, whose unsetting beams
Alone are laved not with the Ocean's streams.

　　Two cities of mankind he wrought.  In one
Marriage was made, and festival went on.
Here brides, environed with bright torches'
　　blaze,

Forth from their bowers they lead, and loudly
  raise
The nuptial chant ; and dancers blithely spring,
Cheered by the sweet-breathed flute and
  harper's string ;
And women at their doors stand wondering.
There, in the market gathered, many stood
Round two contending for the price of blood.
This pleaded he had paid what that one sought,
And each his cause to the tribunal brought.
Each had his eager friends among the crowd,
Whom prudent heralds checked, nor strife
  allowed.
Midway the elders' reverend cirque was shown
Weighing the cause on seats of polished stone;
Each in his hand a sceptre held, and each
Rising pronounced, as came his turn for speech.
Two golden talents in the middle gleamed,
For him, whose sentence wisest should be
  deemed.

  But by the other town besieging sate
Two hosts in shining arms, and held debate
Whether to fire it with the wealth it kept,
Or half as ransom for the rest accept.
But they within, yet unsubdued, prepared

Ambush, their gates committing to the guard
Of women, children, and old men, who all
Stood up for battle on that city's wall.
But to the fray went every fighting man :
Athene and fierce Ares in their van,
With golden arms, in golden raiment trod,
Fair and tall-statured, as becomes the God ;
The people somewhat less.  But when they
    came
Where fitly they their ambuscade might frame,
A pool where drinking cattle oft were found,
Each shining warrior couched upon the ground,
Save two, who posted nigh strict watch did
    keep
For the horned kine approaching with the
    sheep.
They came ; two herdsmen followed them the
    while,
Playing on reeds, unwitting of all guile ;
But they who lay in wait and could foresee
Their coming, sprang from covert suddenly,
And the sleek herds and snowy flocks did hem
Around, and slew the men who tended them.
When then those tarrying in their leaguer
    heard
The clamour by the oxen, each bestirred

Himself unto the rescue, in fleet race
Urging his bounding courser to the place.
And coming to that river-watered lea
They showered their spears, contending despe-
    rately :
And Strife and Tumult warred those men
    among,
And deadly Fate wrought there, and through
    the throng
One wounded, one unhurt, one dead she
    dragged along.
Her garments on her limbs rained bloody
    rain ;
While, figured like to life, they on the plain
The living smote, and struggled for the slain.

Next wrought he a soft fertile fallow-field,
Spacious, that could three annual harvests
    yield ;
And many ploughmen ploughing in it were,
Guiding the yokes of oxen here and there ;
And as each finished his straight furrow's line,
One came forth with a cup of honeyed wine,
And bid him drink ; then turned and drove
    he, fain
The field's extremest limit to attain.

Browner behind him lay the new-turned
    mould,
In colour like the soil, though it of gold
Was wrought in sooth, rare marvel to behold !

Then wrought he a deep field of corn
    embrowned,
Which reapers reaped with sickles ; to the
    ground
The severed ears were falling from their grasp
And binders worked with bands of straw to
    clasp
The ample sheaves ; to whom by boys were
    borne
Armfuls incessant of collected corn.
The lord stood silent, gladdened in his heart
To view the reaping.  'Neath an oak, apart,
Heralds were labouring to equip the feast,
Busy around a huge and slaughtered beast ;
And women, careful of the reapers' weal,
Were kneading the abundant barley-meal.

A vineyard next of gold Hephæstus
    wrought,
With hanging clusters, ripe to blackness,
    fraught.

Silver the stakes that propped the clambering
    vines ;
Blue cyanos the trench ; the hedge's lines
Of tin ; a single narrow path confers
Access upon the thronging vintagers.
Merrily maidens and their youthful mates
Went carrying the sweet fruit in woven
    crates ;
A boy before them, smiting the harp-string,
Made music, with his clear voice carolling
The Linus chant, they, hurrying on the
    sweet
Strain, shouted as they kept due time with
    tripping feet.

A herd of high-horned cattle framed he
    then ;
Part gold, part tin ; they lowing from their
    pen
Impetuously ran forth and straying fed
Where tall reeds trembled in a river's bed.
Four golden herdsmen stoutly strode beside
The herd, by nine swift dogs accompanied.
But two dread lions sprang, and strove to pull
Down, foremost 'mid the kine, a bellowing
    bull.

He, roaring loud, was dragged along, but then
Came to his aid the dogs and active men.
Yet, rending his tough hide, the lions tore
His entrails from him, lapping the black gore.
And vainly sought the herdsmen to pursue,
Encouraging the dogs, that backward drew,
Shunning the strife, yet somewhat close
    remained,
And bayed incessant, but to bite refrained.

   Next, by Hephæstus wrought, the shield
    portrayed
A fair sheep-pasture in a woodland glade ;
And folds, and huts, and stalls o'erroofed he
   made.

   A dance he next designed, such as of old
Dædalus did in ample Gnossus mould
For Ariadne of the lovely hair ;
Mazy and many-mingled.   Dancing there
Moved many a youth, and maid with ardour
   sought
In marriage ; each one with the right hand
   caught
The other's wrist ; garbs of fine linen drest
The comely maids, and each one of the rest

Wore, lustrous as soft oil, a well-spun vest.
A flowery wreath each virgin well beseemed ;
A silver belt, a golden dagger gleamed
On every youth ; and graceful did they run
Nimbly with agile motions every one,
As when a potter whirls his wheel, to try
If, truly wrought, 'twill run round easily ;
And sometimes in encountering files advanced ;
And crowds stood by, beholding them that
    danced
With joy ; to whom a bard began to sing ;
And with them were two tumblers tumbling.

Last, Ocean's strength he made, and with it
    filled
The shining border of the perfect shield.

# Exordium of the Iliad.

SING, Goddess, how Pelides' wrath arose,
    Disastrous, working Greece unnumbered
      woes,
And many a hero's soul to Hades sped,
And glutted dogs and vultures with the dead.
So the design of Zeus was compassed, when
Achilles braved Atrides, king of men.

    What deity the twain in strife engaged?
Leto's bright son, who with the king enraged,
Pestilence dire upon the army brought,
And slew the people, for the king had wrought
Chryses his priest dishonour, what time he
Came suing for his daughter's liberty.
To the swift vessels came he, in his hand
Apollo's laurel on a golden wand,
And, proffering noble gifts, entreaty made
To all, but most the two Atridæ prayed :—

    "Atridæ twain, and well-mailed Grecians all,
To you, by Heaven's decree, may it befall
To raze the towers of Troy, and o'er the main
Returning, greet your native land again.

But for this ransom yield my child to me,
Revering the far-darting Deity."

  Then did the Greeks, applauding, sentence
    give,
The priest to honour, and his gifts receive.
This only Agamemnon could not brook,
But quelled the suppliant with austere re-
    buke :—

"Let me not find thee by the vessels black,
Old man, or lingering now, or venturing back,
Else little profit will, I ween, to thee
Apollo's sceptre and his laurel be.
Her I release not, whom till grey and old,
Argos, far-sundered from her home, shall hold,
Meek vassal of my couch and loom. Thou cease,
Nor move my wrath, while hence thou mayest
    in peace."

  He spoke, the old man trembled and obeyed ;
Silent by the loud-roaring sea he strayed :
Then, at a distance, lifted up his prayer
To King Apollo, sprung from Leto fair :—
"God of the silver bow, thy servant hear.
Hear, Sminthian, thou whom Chryse doth
    revere,
And Tenedos, and Cilla the divine.

If ever I have garlanded thy shrine,
If ever I have burned acceptably
Fat thighs of bullocks and of goats to thee ;
Accomplish thou this my petition, may
Greece for my anguish by thine arrows pay."

Thus he lamenting, him Apollo heard,
And from Olympus' summit at the word
Descended, deadly ire embosoming.
His bow and teeming quiver did he fling
Across his shoulders ; fearfully the load
Of arrows rattled on the angry God
Striding in the similitude of night.
Down sat he, and dispersed his arrows' might.
Dire was the twanging of the silver bow.
First mules and dogs the incessant shafts laid
    low,
But soon the troops, and thicker hour by hour
Blazed the appalling flames that did the dead
    devour.
Nine days he hurled his arrows at the fleet,
The tenth, Achilles bade the people meet
In council.   Hera did the thought instil,
For much it pitied her to see their ill.
When then together all were gathered
Achilles swift of foot arose and said.

# The Encounter of the Hosts.

AS when on some loud coast the wind impels
  The thronging waters, vast the billow
    swells,
And o'er all other sea a moment towers,
Then, furiously flung forward on the shores,
Curves its surmounting crest, and far away
Hurls with a roar the lavish-scattered spray :
So streamed in one huge host the gathered
    bands
Of Greeks incessant to the war.   Commands
Their leaders gave ; silently moved along
The others ; dumb seemed all that serried
    throng,
So deep the awe their chieftains did inspire :
They marched, and as they marched their
    armour flashed forth fire.
But as when, gathered in a rich man's stall,
Unnumbered ewes stand at the milking, all
With ceaseless bleats replying to their young,
Uproar prevailed the Trojan host among ;

From various lands, of stranger tribes who
    came,
Unlike their accent, nor their speech the same.
Their bosoms blazed with fire from Ares
    caught ;
Like passion mid the Greeks Athene wrought:
And Terror stalked around, and with him
    Dread ;
And Strife insatiate mid the armies sped,
Sister and mate of Ares, who appears
Pigmy at first, then on the sudden rears
Her head in heaven's eminence, while yet
Her feet upon the nether earth are set.
There mid the hosts woe-working was she
    found,
Strewing the fire of battle all around.

# The Trojan Camp at Night.

BUT they, full of high thoughts, by battle's
    gate,
Burning huge fires, all night encamping sate;
As when the bright stars gloriously gird
The radiant moon, and Æther sleeps unstirred.
And boldly stand forth headland, cliff and
    grove,
And heaven immeasurable is rent above,
And every constellation manifest,
And gladness fills the gazing shepherd's
    breast :
So many fires 'twixt stream and navy shone,
Before the massy walls of Ilion—
A thousand fires !  By each, upon the plain,
Sat fifty warriors, flashing forth again
Fire from their arms, and, champing the
    white corn,
Their steeds stood by the cars, awaiting fair-
    throned Morn.

# Poseidon goes to the aid of the Greeks.

ZEUS, having led up Hector and his might
      Unto the navy, left them there to fight
Incessantly with toil and wail of war,
But turned himself his radiant eyes afar ;
The many-steeded plains of Thrace he scanned,
And close-ranked Mysians, fighters hand to
      hand ;
The milk-fed Hippomolgians viewed he then.
And Abii, most just of mortal men.
But unto Ilion looked he not at all,
Not deeming that it ever could befall
That any God would aid or those who bled
For Troy, or who against her combated.

   But great Poseidon kept not watch in vain.
Marvelling he marked the battle on the plain,
Throned upon Samothrace's woody crest,
Whence was the whole of Ida manifest,
And Troy's towers and the navy clear-exprest.
There sat he, risen from the main's profound,

Grieving to see his Grecians giving ground,
And greatly wroth with Zeus.   Sudden at last
He rose, and swiftly down the steep he passed;
The  mountain  trembled  with  each  step  he
    took,
The forest with the quaking  mountain shook.
Three strides he made, and with the fourth he
    stood
At Ægæ, where is  founded 'neath the flood
His hall of glorious gold that cannot fade;
Entering therein, beneath the yoke he laid
His steeds  with  feet  of  brass  and  manes  of
    gold,
Swift as the wind, and his own frame did fold
In golden weeds, and grasped within his hand
The  well-wrought  golden  scourge,  and  took
    his stand
Behind the coursers, and immediately
Wended upon the surface of the sea;
And all the whales and  monsters knew their
    king,
And rose up from the bottom frolicing;
And the sea's face was parted with a smile,
And rapidly the horses sped the while;
The brazen axle was not wet below;
And to the Grecian navy did they go.

# Achilles recovers the Body of Patroclus.

THESE words swift Iris spake, then flew above,
And straight uprose the chieftain dear to Jove.
Divine Athene on his shoulders laid
Her many-tasselled ægis, and displayed
A gold cloud round his head, and caused intense
Effusion of bright fire to issue thence.
And as aërial flame is seen afar,
Ascending from some isle where men of war
Have all day long assailed with shafts and spears
The lone and unassisted islanders,
But at sunsetting these along their shores
Light frequent beacons ; swift the signal soars,
Summoning their neighbours in fleet ships to speed

Thither, and bring them succour in their
    need ;
Thus streamed the splendour of Achilles' brow
To heaven, as he arose and stood below
Behind the trench, nor with the rest did
    stand,
Observant of his mother's wise command.
He stood and shouted.   Pallas too did swell
His shout with hers, and straight unutterable
Tumult and terror on the Trojans fell.
And as when loud war-music thrilling clear
Rings from the clarion of a trumpeter
When a town's walls are circuited with foes,
So thrillingly Achilles' voice arose.
When then their ears rang with that brazen
    shout
Great dread fell on them all, the steeds about
Turned with the chariots, for they did fore-
    cast
Ruin, and they that drove beheld aghast
The fire that unabatingly was shed
By Pallas from Æacides's head.
Thrice did Achilles lift his voice's might,
Thrice Trojans and allies recoiled in flight,
And twelve great champions, famous in the
    wars,

Died, pierced by their own spears and crushed
    by their own cars.
But, triumphing, the Greeks Patroclus dead
Drew from amid the javelins ; on a bed
Bestowed the corpse ; and every Myrmidon
Stood by it, weeping bitter tears thereon.
Sadly mid these Achilles also bent,
Wailing his mate beloved, gory and rent,
Stretched on the bier, whom he himself had
    sent
With his own car and coursers to the plain,
But not with them had welcomed back again.

# *Achilles arms Himself.*

EAGER Athene thus did Zeus incite
    Yet more, from heaven she suddenly took
    flight ;
In figure like an osprey long of wing
She darted where the Greeks apparelling
Themselves   in   arms   were   stationed,   there
    imbued
Achilles' breast with nectar, lest he should
Faint in the battle, for refreshment fain,
Then flew up to her father's dome again :
But from the ships they poured and swarmed
    upon the plain
And thick as Zeus' cold flakes, when forth they
    fare,
Borne of the north wind through the crystal
    air,
Legions innumerable landward flowed
Of many-glancing helms, and mail that glowed
With over-lapping plates, and bossy shields,

And ashen spears.　Their splendour from the
　　fields
Flashed up to heaven, and all the earth about
Laughed luminous with lustre they cast out,
And quaked beneath the infinite footfall,
And high Achilles armed him 'mid them all.
Raging he gnashed his teeth, flame in his eye
Lightened, but on his heart weighed misery ;
And wrath and sadness shared him as he
　　stood,
And bright Hephæstus' battle-garb indued.
First in his greaves his legs he did enclasp,
Well riveting the silver ankle-hasp ;
His bosom in his cuirass next arrayed ;
Then hung his shining silver-studded blade
Over his shoulder ; then his shield he took,
Massy and huge ; whose beam was as the look
Of the broad moon from heaven ; or as when
Fire blazes on the hills where shepherds pen
Their flocks at night, and splendour streams
　　to sea,
Discerned of them who toss unhappily
On the great waters, who may not arrive
At land, but with the wind unwilling drive ;
Such light the fair elaborate buckler shed.
Then his huge crested helmet on his head—

Which shone as if a star his brows had
  crowned—
He set, and all the golden plumes around
Danced thrilling, on the helm by deft He-
  phæstus bound.
Then did he prove the armour, if it might
Be truly fashioned, fitting him aright,
And felt as he were winged with feathers
  light,
So aptly did it sheathe him.  Next the spear
He grasped which Peleus anciently did bear,
Tough, long, and heavy, which not anyone
Of Greeks could brandish, saving him alone ;
The shaft by Chiron felled on Pelion, then
To Peleus given, doom to warrior men.
But Alcimus and bold Automedon
Wrought by the steeds, fitting the harness
  on.
The horses' mouths with curbs they did con-
  strain,
And to the chariot seat drew back the rein.
Automedon then mounted, in his right
Shaking the beaming scourge.  As sunshine
  bright,
Godlike Achilles sprang unto his side,
And loudly to his father's coursers cried :

" Xanthus and Balius, Podarge's breed,
Bring ye this day your lord with better speed
Back from the field, when from the field ye
    fare,
Nor leave him, as ye left Patroclus, there."


But to him audibly his steed thus said,
Swift Xanthus, from the chariot, as his head
He on a sudden drooped, and with his mane,
Unloosened from the yoke-band, swept the
    plain—
For white-armed Hera gave him voice—"This
    day,
Achilles, we shall save thee from the fray ;
But nigh at hand the hour when thou must
    fall,
For which accuse not thou thy steeds at all,
But Gods, and Fates who life and death dis-
    pense.
Not by our tardiness or indolence
Did Trojans strip the arms Patroclus wore,
But the bright God whom fair-haired Leto
    bore
Slew him amongst the first, yet Hector won
The glory.  Fleet may we as Zephyr run,
Who fleetest among winds is famed to be,

Yet slaughter and the slayers wait for thee,
Whom shall a mortal slay, and eke a Deity."

   Here ceased he, for his tongue the Furies
     tied :
To him Achilles wrathfully replied,
" Xanthus, why bode my death ? thou need'st
     not so ;
That I must perish here full well I know,
Far from my father, from my mother far ;
Yet verily I will not cease from war
Till I have overthrown the Trojans quite."

   He said, and shouting drove into the fight.

## The Gods join in the Battle.

BUT to the Gods, coming where strove these
    men,
Came strife, and with the rest they battled then.
And with a mighty voice Athene cried,
Now where the moat the rampart fortified
Shouting, and now the roaring main beside.
Ares upon his part, as storms a blast,
Now crying to the Trojans his voice cast
Forth from the citadel, and now where is
Callicolone by swift Simois.

Thus cheered they on the armies, their own
    might
Mingling with theirs in formidable fight.
And Zeus the sire of Gods and men dismayed
The heavens with thunder, and Poseidon made
Tremor in all the immeasurable earth,
And Ida where the many springs have birth
Quaked with her peak and every mountain-
    spur,

And Troy's towers and the navy quaked with
    her.
And nether Hades, despot of the dead,
Leapt from his throne and cried aloud, in dread
Lest earth should yawn, so strong Poseidon
    shook,
And suffer men and heavenly Gods to look
Into the squalor of his realm unblest,
Which even the undying Gods detest.

# Idyllic.

# The Cyclop.

OINTMENT, or pill, or potion cannot be,
　　So I opine, of love the remedy :
Solely the Muse can soothe the amorous mind ;
Sweet is her antidote, but hard to find.
Thou, Nicias, best canst tell if this be true,
Beloved of Muses, and physician too.

Such comfort did, at least, the Muse provide
For Polypheme, my countryman one-eyed,
Whose love for wave-born Galate appeared
Twin with his young contemporary beard.
Now be it known that when a Cyclop pines,
'Tis not his wont to woo with valentines,
But with distraction.　Oft-times, having fed,
Homeward would wend his flock unshepherded,
While sole beside the weedy shore sat he,
Languishing for the love of Galate,
From morn to eve ; so rankled the dire dart
By Eros deep implanted in his heart ;
Yet solace found, as, looking to the main,

E

From a high rock he thus poured forth his
strain :—

"Than calves more skittish, than unripened
fruit
Of vines more harsh, why, Galate, my suit
Dost thou reject, and, as the sheep doth fly
The haggard wolf, avoid me : when my eye
Slumber hath sealed, emerging from the
main ;
When I am wakened speeding back again ?

"When had my passion birth ?  When thou
didst come
And our rough mountain with my mother
roam,
Seeking for hyacinths, I showed the way,
And ne'er have discontinued to this day
Burning for thee, but much thou car'st for
this.
Full well I know whence thy aversion is ;
Merely because my shaggy eyebrow goes
Right on from ear to ear, while 'neath it
glows
One solitary eye, a sight uncouth,
And my broad nose is almost in my mouth.

Most trivial cause, thee from thy swain to
    keep!
One eyebrow have I, but a thousand sheep,
Which milking, I exhaust the foaming pail.
On cheese at every season I regale,
My crates being always loaded. On the reed
All other Cyclop minstrels I exceed,
And thereupon my passion oft-times vent,
Hymning our loves till night is well-nigh
    spent.
Nay, more, for thee my thoughtful fondness
    rears
Eleven collared fawns, and four young bears.
Come—thou wilt not regret it. Let blue sea
Break on its shingly beach, unheard by thee:
More sweetly wilt thou slumber in my cave,
And arms, dear pet. There laurels richly
    wave,
Blent with slim cypress, and dark ivy-twines
Creep interlaced with purple-fruited vines;
And, cold from woody Ætna's peak of snow,
Water delicious doth beside them flow;
Who could prefer the sea, these things being
    so?
Am I too shaggy for thy taste? I lay
Great store of timber by, and fire for aye

Smouldering 'neath ashes. Take thyself a
    brand,
And singe these whiskers with thy lovely
    hand ;
Yea, even my very soul, if this thou crave,
Or my one eye, best treasure that I have.
Were I but born with gills ! so might I dive
Downward to thee, and thus thy hand
    contrive
To kiss, thy sweeter lips prohibited,
And bring thee lilies white, or poppies red
(Those bloom in summer, these in winter
    weather—
'Tis clear I could not bring them both to-
    gether).
Yet will I the next mariner beseech
Whom traffic brings us here, and he shall
    teach
The swimmer's mystery, that I may prove
If deeps have aught, excepting thee, to love.
Come, forth my Galatea, from the spray,
Come and forget, as I, the homeward way.
Come feed with me my sheep upon the leas,
Milk my full ewes, and make with rennet
    cheese.
Most do I blame my mother, for indeed

Ne'er in my favour will she intercede,
Though seeing me grow thinner day by day:
But I'll be even with her, for I'll say
My feet are swelled, and of my head complain,
And make her thus participate my pain.

"O Cyclop, Cyclop, much wool-gathering !
Get to thy cave, plait wicker there, or bring
Young branches for thy lambs, 'twere far more
    wise.
Milk thou the ewe thou hast, leave her that
    flies.
Some fairer Galatea wilt thou meet.
Oft maidens at the evening hour entreat
My company to play with them, and all
When I comply, straightway a-laughing fall :
On land, 'tis clear, our credit is not small."

Thus warbling, did our Polypheme appease
His amorous woe, and save his doctor's fees.

# The Fishermen.

POVERTY, Diophantus, can alone
  Awake invention ; 'tis by her is shown
How toil must be relieved, 'tis she can keep
The weary labourer even from his sleep ;
Or, if a little while at rest he lies,
Trouble is soon at hand to bid him rise.

Two aged fishers in a wattled shed
Rested together on the couch they spread
Of withered leaves and moss.  By them were
    laid
The tokens of their poverty and trade :
Baskets, rods, hooks, baits bedded in sea-weed,
Lines, wickers, nets, traps twined from rush
    and reed,
A pair of oars, on props a boat decayed.
A mat for either head scant pillow made,
A cloak was either's quilt.  Not great their
    store,
But when did ever fishermen have more ?
No bolt their cabin had, no dog ; indeed,
Their penury dispensed them from the need ;

Nor neighbour had they any, save the sea
Moaning and rolling everlastingly,
Close by the crazy cot.  Not yet the clear
Moon had fulfilled the half of her career,
When, roused by need, they woke, their cares
    began
To soothe with talk, and thus one fisher-
    man :—

### First Fisherman.

'Tis certain they must lie, my friend, who say
That summer nights decrease with lengthen-
    ing day ;
Ten thousand dreams I've dreamed, nor yet
    the sun
Is risen ; will the night be never done ?

### Second Fisherman.

Rashly thou blam'st fair summer, time of all
Fittest for fishing.  It doth not befall
Night to transgress her limits, but the throng
Of cares persuades thee to esteem her long.

### First Fisherman.

Canst thou interpret dreams ?  This night
    to me
A rare one came, which I'll impart to thee ;

Our visions like our fish divided be ;
And thou will tell me why it came, and
    whence ;
The better half of prophecy is sense.
Leisure have we ; how else, the sea beside,
Can slumber's gaps be better occupied ?
And wakeful as a nightingale at night,
Or as the lamp perpetually bright
In the town hall, am I.

### SECOND FISHERMAN.

            Come then, and tell
What was this visionary miracle.

### FIRST FISHERMAN.

When yester eve, o'ercome with toils marine,
I slept (not full ; our meal, thou know'st, had
    been
Early and scant), methought I watchful sate
Perched on a rock, dangling deceitful bait
Into the sea (such dreams our day prepares :
Fishers must dream of fish, as hounds of
    hares).
A huge fish bit, was firmly hooked ; well-nigh,
Plunging, he snapped the bended rod that I
Held with both hands, with all the skill I had

Playing him, fearful, for the hook was bad.
Now slow I pulled, and let him feel the pain,
Now slacked the line, now tightened it again ;
At length prevailed, and, marvel to behold !
Drew from the deep a fish of solid gold.
And much I feared lest peradventure he
Some favourite of the monarch of the sea,
Or azure Amphitrite's pet might be :
Yet not the less him from the angle took,
Gently, lest gold should cleave unto the hook ;
And towed him happily to land, and swore
Devoutly I would go to sea no more,
But stay on land, and lord it with my gold ;
And then I woke, and now my dream is told.
But thou advise me, friend, for I am loth
To go to sea, lest I should break my oath.

### SECOND FISHERMAN.

Nay, friend, your scruple is but a mistake :
You caught no fish, and so no oath can
    break.
Dreams are but lies, yet to your promise hold
So far as it concerns the fish of gold ;
But seek the fish of flesh, or like it seems
That you will starve amid your golden dreams.

# Spring. From Meleager.

WINDS sleep, snows melt, the sea's revolt is
    quelled,
The blue of heaven unveiled, and Spring
    beheld,
Scattering glad boons, a bright and fair-robed
    thing,
Whose path is life, as o'er the carpeting
Of emerald earth she wends with gracious
    tread.
Now leaves transparent in soft light are
    spread
Forth from the quickening branch that sways
    and droops
With blossom ; now the meadows bloom with
    troops
Of meek and pastoral flowers, where sits in
    peace
The shepherd piping for his flock's increase.
The ports are void, the issuing vessels strew
A moving whiteness o'er the mirroring blue.

With shouts and thrilling laughter, o'er the
    sod
Bounding, the ivied Bacchante hails her God.
Forth sally the thick bees, the feathery crowds
Assemble on the branch, or from high clouds
The note descends ; the river teems with
    swans ;
The thatch her swallow harbours ; halcyons
Talk softly to the sea ; and brake and dell
Sequester the sweet throat of Philomel.
Then, if the leaf be new, the bare earth clad,
The flock prolific, and the shepherd glad,
Furrowed the sea, and Bacchus served with
    songs,
The hive astir, the air with winged throngs
Peopled, and music breathed from every tree,
Silent alone and thankless shall he be
Whose gift 'mid mortal men is melody ?
Nay, rather let him smite his lyre and sing
Hymns with a happy heart to genial Spring.

# *From Moschus.*

WHEN gentle winds but ruffle the calm sea
  My breast courageous grows, and earth
    to me
Dear as enticing Ocean cannot be :
But when the great main roars, and white
    with foam
Huge waves tower up from it, and bellowing
    come
To burst on land, I wistful seek a home
In groves retired, where, when the storm
    descends,
It brings but music to the pine it bends.
Unblest, whose house the wandering billows
    bear
With them, who strive with sea for fishy fare.
But I beneath the broad-leaved plane will lie,
Where some bright fountain, breaking forth
    hard by,
Delights and not disturbs with bubbling
    melody.

# From Bion.

YOUNG was I when I saw fair Venus stand
Before me, leading in her lovely hand
Eros, whose drooping eye the herbage sought,
And thus, "Dear herdsman, let my child be
taught
Music by thee," therewith she went away.
Then did I in all innocence essay
To teach, as though he would have learned of
me
The sources of sweet-flowing melody :
Pan's pipe and Pallas' flute, how Hermes
bade
The tortoise sing, and how Apollo made
The cittern.  But, not heeding mine a whit,
He sang himself a song, and taught me it—
*How Venus reigns, and all in heaven above*
*And land and sea is subject unto Love.*
And I forgot all I to Love did tell,
But all he taught me I remember well.

# From the Same.

ALONE of all, the Muses do not fear
    Eros, but love, and joy to have him near ;
And him, who sings by Eros unsubdued,
They shun, and hence his strain is wild and
    rude ;
But he who sings as Eros doth persuade,
The Muses' minstrel also shall be made.
Witness myself, for when I seek to sing
Of any mortal or immortal thing
Save Love, my song expires in stammering.
But when of love, or one beloved by me,
Spontaneous streams the might of melody.

# From Macho.

PHILOXENUS the bard, report assures,
　　Was ranked the paragon of epicures.
One day a huge and special fish he got
(If dory or if lamprey, fame says not),
And made one meal of it, except the head,
Then, with good cause, betook himself to bed,
And for the doctor sent. The leech with speed
Arrived, examined, pondered, and decreed :
" As near as Hippocratic art can fix,
You'll die at five, perhaps it may be six,
Improve the span allotted, say your prayers,
Send for your friends, and settle your affairs."
" Thanks, leech," the patient said, " but you
　　must know
My testament was sealed some time ago.
Bacchus and Venus have I served with heed,
And with the other Gods have well agreed :
Phœbus will guard my laurels, if attacked :
My copyrights are settled by the Act.

Then, since fell Fate, with her abhorrèd shears,
Slits the frail tissue of my mortal years,
And Charon calls, that I may die resigned,
In peace and charity with all mankind,
And nothing may regret, nor aught may wish ;
Just send me up the remnant of that fish."

# *Melinno's Ode to Rome.*

HAIL, child of Mars ! to whom alone
   The Gods with equal hands have given
Earth for a kingdom, yet a throne
   Stable as heaven.

To thee most ancient Fate allowed
   A destiny unshared, to be
A Queen unburdened and unbowed
   By royalty.

Earth's neck is bended to thy yoke,
   Thy bands her mighty bosom span.
The hoar Sea quivers at thy stroke,
   Pilot of Man !

And Time that doth to all allot,
   Save thee, brief date and various day,
To thee alone awardeth not
   Change or decay.